Animal Stories

WRITTEN BY
Lucy Kincaid

ILLUSTRATED BY
Tom Hirst

B R I M A X

MIRANDA IS LOST

Miranda Goose is always dreaming.
She dreams when she is asleep.
She dreams when she is awake.
She walks with her head in the air.
She forgets to look where she is
going.
"Look at Miranda," say the hens.
"Look at Miranda," say the ducks.
"Look at Miranda," says the cat.
"She is dreaming," says the dog.

Miranda's head is in the air.
She does not see the gate.
She does not know it is open.
She walks out of the farmyard.
Everyone is busy.
No one sees Miranda go.

"Where is Miranda?" say the hens.
"Where is Miranda?" say the ducks.
"I cannot see her anywhere," says the cat.
"She is lost," says the dog.
"We must find Miranda," say the hens.
"Look!" say the ducks.
It is a footprint.
"It is a clue," says the cat.

13

There are some more footprints.
"Let us follow them," says the
dog.
The dog follows the footprints.
The hens follow the dog.
The ducks follow the hens.
The cat follows the ducks.

Miranda is still walking.
She has walked a long way.
Her head is in the air.
She is looking at the clouds.
She is singing about clouds.
"Tra la, tra la,
Little clouds
So fluffy and soft
Tra la, tra la."

The footprints lead to the meadow. The grass is long.
It is hiding the hens.
It is hiding the ducks.
They are not lost.
They are following the dog.
The cat is following behind.
"There is Miranda," says the dog.
"We can see her," say the hens.
"So can we," say the ducks.
"What is she doing?" asks the cat.

Miranda is not looking up.
Miranda is looking down.
She is looking at her feet.
She is surprised.
She is in the stream.
"How did I get here?" she asks herself.
She looks all around.
"I am lost," says Miranda.
"I want to go home."

"How did you find me?" asks Miranda.

"We followed your footprints," says the dog.

"We will take you home," say her friends.

The dog leads the way.

The ducks follow the dog.

The hens follow the ducks.

Miranda follows the hens.

The cat follows Miranda.

Miranda is back home.
Miranda's head is in the air.
She is dreaming.
"The gate is open," say the hens.
"She will get lost again," say the ducks.
"We must close the gate," says the cat.
"I will do it," says the dog.
Now Miranda is safe.

Can you find five differences between the two pictures?

26

Can you say these words and find them in the picture?

pink hat

bucket

duck

Miranda

MIRANDA AND THE FROGS

Miranda is on the pond. She has her head in the air. She has her feet in the water. She is dreaming. Miranda dreams all the time. Miranda is paddling her feet. The frog is having fun. He is holding on to Miranda's foot. Miranda does not notice what the frog is doing.

Miranda has finished swimming.
She is climbing out of the pond.
The frog is sitting on her foot.
Miranda is still dreaming. She does
not know what the frog is doing.
Miranda is looking at the clouds.
The frog is having a ride.

33

"Can I come too?" asks his friend.
"Hop aboard!" says the frog to his friend.
What a bumpy ride it is!
"Hold on tight," says the frog.
"I am holding on tight," says his friend.

"Look at the frogs!" say the hens.
"Look at the frogs!" say the ducks.
"Look at the frogs!" says the cat.
"Look at your feet, Miranda!" says
the dog.

Miranda hears the dog. She stops dreaming. She looks down. She can only see her toes. She cannot see her feet. The frogs are still having fun.

Miranda lifts up her foot. The frogs hop onto the other foot. "I cannot see any frogs," says Miranda. She puts her foot down. She lifts up the other foot. The frogs hop back again. They are having fun.

39

"I cannot see any frogs," says Miranda.

"Shake your foot," say the hens.

"Shake your foot," say the ducks.

"Shake your foot," says the cat.

Miranda lifts up her foot. She shakes it.

"Now shake the other one," says the dog.

So Miranda does.

"Be quick. Jump off!" says the frog to his friend.

They are too late. Miranda shakes her foot. The frogs fall off in a heap. The frogs are laughing. They are not hurt. The frogs are having fun.

"Now I can see the frogs," says Miranda.

Miranda has not got her head in the air. Miranda is looking down. Miranda is watching her feet. Miranda is looking for frogs. Miranda is not looking where she is going. She bumps into the wall. She falls head over tail.

Miranda picks herself up.

"Put your head in the air," say the hens.

"Look at the sky," say the ducks.

"Forget about your feet," says the cat.

"Carry on dreaming," says the dog.

So Miranda does. The dog sends the frogs back to the pond.

Can you find five differences between the two pictures?

48   The gate is open, not closed.   5. The frog is on Miranda's other foot.
1. The bucket is missing.   2. There is an extra flower.   3. There is a different bird on the wall.
4.

Can you say these words and find them in the picture?

frog

foot

wall

pond

49

MIRANDA GOOSE

Miranda is always dreaming. She forgets to look where she is going. The hens keep out of her way. The ducks keep out of her way. The cat keeps out of her way. The dog keeps out of her way.

"Who is that?" say the hens.

"Who is that?" say the ducks.

"Who is that?" says the cat.

There is another goose in the farmyard.

They know it is not Miranda.
"It is a visitor," says the dog.
Miranda has her head in the air.
She is dreaming. She does not see
the visitor. The visitor has HIS
head in the air. He is dreaming
too. HE does not see Miranda.
Everyone is looking.

Will Miranda bump into the visitor? Will the visitor bump into Miranda? The hens close their eyes. The ducks close their eyes. The cat closes her eyes. The dog keeps his eyes open. He wants to see what happens. Miranda is very close to the visitor. The visitor is very close to Miranda. They are almost touching. Everyone holds their breath. What will happen?

"Look out!" shout the hens.
"Look out!" shout the ducks.
"Look out!" shouts the cat.
"Look out!" shouts the dog.
They are all too late! Miranda
thinks they are shouting at
someone else. The visitor thinks
they are shouting at someone else.
There is a collision! Miranda's feet
are in the air. The visitor's feet are
in the air.

"How did that happen?" asks Miranda.

"I don't know," says the visitor.

"You must look where you are going or it will happen again," says the dog.

Miranda picks herself up. The visitor picks himself up.

"Please look where you are going," says Miranda.

"I will if YOU will," says the visitor.

It did not take them long to forget. Miranda is looking at the clouds again. The visitor is dreaming with his eyes closed. There is going to be another collision!

"Stop them!" shout the hens.

"Stop them!" shout the ducks.

"Stop them!" shouts the cat.

"Hold on to their tails!" shouts the dog.

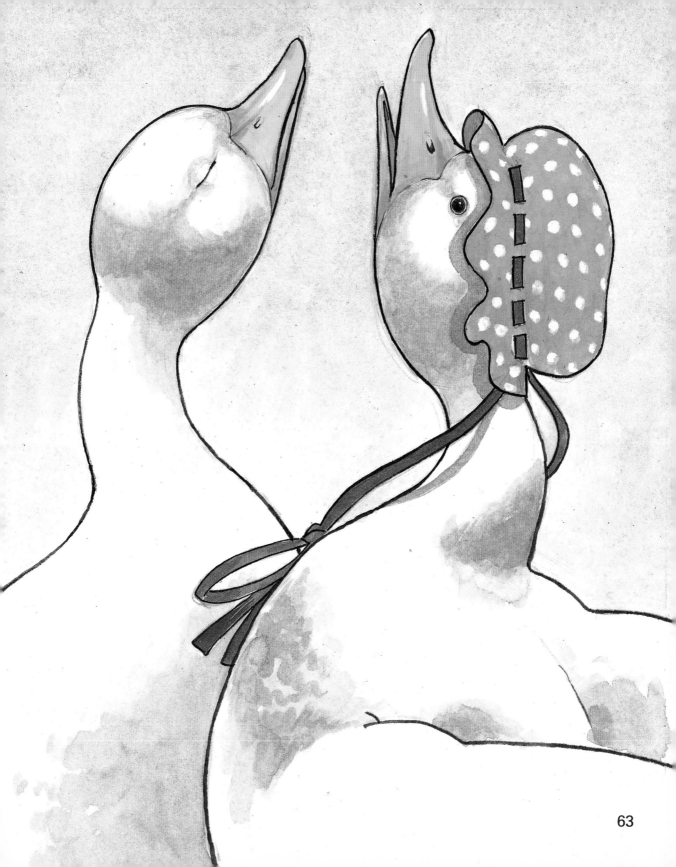

Miranda stops looking at the clouds. The visitor opens his eyes. They stop. They have to stop. Someone is pulling on their tails. Their chins are touching. But they have not bumped into each other. What a narrow escape!

Miranda's tail is sore. The visitor's tail is sore.

"It is not safe here anymore," says the visitor. "I am going home. I will dream in my own farmyard."

"What a good idea!" says the dog.

"One dreaming goose is enough for any farmyard," says the cat.
"I agree," says the dog.
"It was exciting for a while," say the ducks.
"We are glad nobody pulled our tails," say the hens.
Miranda is busy with a new dream. She does not say anything at all.

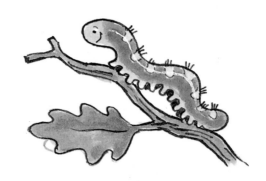

Can you find five differences between the two pictures?

1. The ball is blue, not red.   2. The hens are in a different place.   3. There are two butterflies, not one.   4. The pigs' feeding trough is missing.   5. Miranda is looking the opposite way.

Can you say these words and find them in the picture?

another goose

piglet

gate

bird

MIRANDA
FINDS A BELL

Miranda Goose is always dreaming.
She dreams when she is asleep.
She dreams when she is awake.
She walks with her head in the air.
She forgets to look where she is going.

75

Miranda doesn't see the ducks.
She almost steps on them.
The ducks jump out of her way.
The ducks bump into each other.
"Quack! Quack!" say the ducks.
The ducks are angry.
"I'm sorry," says Miranda.
Miranda does not see the cat.
She steps on the cat's tail.
"Meow!" says the cat.
The cat is angry.
"I'm sorry," says Miranda.

Miranda does not see the hens.
She knocks over their water.
She spills their food.
"Cluck! Cluck!" say the hens.
The hens are angry.
"I'm sorry," says Miranda.
Miranda does not see the dog.
But the dog tries to get out of her
way. He bumps into the cat.
"Meow!" says the cat.
"I'm sorry," says the dog.

Everyone tries to keep out of Miranda's way. They end up bumping into each other.
What a mess!
The ducks quack. The hens cluck.
The cat meows. The dog barks.
Miranda looks surprised.
"We must do something to stop this," says the dog. "Or someone will get hurt."
"We must have a meeting right now," say the ducks.

Miranda has her head in the air.
She is not looking where she is
going. She does not see the
meeting. She walks into the middle
of it. What a mess!

"How did that happen?" asks
Miranda.

"You weren't looking where you
were going," says the dog.

"I'm sorry," says Miranda.

"I will try not to do it again."

Miranda does try. She tries very hard.

But she still walks with her head in the air.

No one is safe. Everyone jumps out of her way when they can. But sometimes they are busy. They do not see her coming.

Miranda has her head in the air.
She sees a bell on a ribbon.
It is caught in a bush.
"I have found some treasure," says
Miranda.
She pushes her head through the
loop of the ribbon. The bell hangs
round her neck like a necklace.

Ting-a-ling! Ting-a-ling!

"What is that noise?" say the hens.

"It's Miranda," say the ducks.

"We can hear her coming," says the cat.

"We can get out of her way before she bumps into us," says the dog.

Now it is safe in the farmyard.
No one is stepped on. No one is
bumped into. Nothing gets spilled.
Now Miranda can walk with her
head in the air and dream all day
long. Everyone is safe. Everyone is
happy.

Can you find five differences between the two pictures?

1. There is an extra flower.   2. Miranda's bell is missing.   3. The dog is standing, not sitting.   4. The ducks are talking to the hens, not the cat.   5. The butterfly is missing.

Can you say these words and find them in the picture?

bell

rabbit

butterfly

flower